PICTURE DAY
JITTERS

PICTURE DAY
JITTERS

JULIE DANNEBERG

ILLUSTRATED BY JUDY LOVE

iɴi Charlesbridge

For teachers everywhere. Thanks for helping to hold the world together.—J. D.

For the dedicated photographers who chronicle our school years in tiny paper memories.—J. L.

Text copyright © 2022 by Julie Danneberg
Illustrations copyright © 2022 by Judy Love

At the time of publication, all URLs printed in this book were accurate and active. Charlesbridge, the author, and the illustrator are not responsible for the content or accessibility of any website.

Published by Charlesbridge
9 Galen Street
Watertown, MA 02472
(617) 926-0329
www.charlesbridge.com

Library of Congress Cataloging-in-Publication Data
Names: Danneberg, Julie, 1958– author. | Love, Judith DuFour, illustrator.
Title: Picture day jitters / Julie Danneberg; illustrated by Judy Love.
Description: Watertown, MA: Charlesbridge, [2022] | Audience: Ages 6–9. | Audience: Grades 2–3. | Summary: "It is class picture day and Mrs. Hartwell is doing her best to keep her class looking their neat and well-dressed best, but as the hours pass the students become messier and messier. By picture time at the end of the day, they look like their normal selves—and that works out just fine."—Provided by publisher.
Identifiers: LCCN 2021029119 (print) | LCCN 2021029120 (ebook) | ISBN 9781623541576 (hardcover) | ISBN 9781623543877 (softcover) | ISBN 9781632899415 (ebook)
Subjects: LCSH: Teachers—Juvenile fiction. | Photographs—Juvenile fiction. | Schools—Juvenile fiction. | CYAC: Teachers—Fiction. | Photographs—Fiction. | Schools—Fiction. | LCGFT: Picture books.
Classification: LCC PZ7.D2327 Pi 2022 (print) | LCC PZ7.D2327 (ebook) | DDC [E]—dc23
LC record available at https://lccn.loc.gov/2021029119
LC ebook record available at https://lccn.loc.gov/2021029120

Printed in China
(hc) 10 9 8 7 6 5 4 3 2 1
(pb) 10 9 8 7 6 5 4 3 2 1

Illustrations done in watercolor, transparent dyes, and India ink on Strathmore paper
Display type set in Lunchbox by Kimmy Designs
Text type set in Electra by Adobe Systems Incorporated
Color separations by Boston Photo Imaging, Boston, MA
Printed by 1010 Printing International Limited in Huizhou, Guangdong, China
Production supervision by Jennifer Most Delaney
Designed by Diane M. Earley

At the end of the day on Tuesday, Mrs. Hartwell reminded her class that school pictures were the next day. "Don't forget to look your best," she said as they headed out the door.

The next morning during circle time,
Alexandra asked, "How do we look?"
   "You look picture-perfect!" Mrs. Hartwell said.
   The class smiled.
   "So do you," said Arianna.

"Now, let's see if we can all stay that way. Our class pictures aren't until the end of the day," Mrs. Hartwell told them.

The class frowned.

"You can do it," she assured them. But inside she knew that this was going to be a very, very, very long day.

Morning math class passed quickly. Mrs. Hartwell was surprised by how messy fractions could be.

"That's okay. I can fix it," she told them.
And she did.

Next was morning recess. The students got to
go outside, but there was no chalk, no chasing,
no digging, and definitely no fun.

By the time morning recess was over, everyone still looked picture-perfect. For the most part.

Writing workshop went pretty well,
until the pencil sharpener broke.
It was nice of Amir to clean it up.
     But it was messy. And now Amir
was messy, too.

"That's okay," Mrs. Hartwell said. "I can fix it."
And she did.

Mrs. Hartwell decided that maybe it would be a good idea for everyone to eat lunch in the classroom.

"And then we can play quiet games at our seats. Won't that be fun?" she asked.

The class didn't look too sure.

Mrs. Hartwell forgot that some of her students could get messy even when sitting quietly in their seats.

"Don't worry, I can fix it," she said.

After lunch, the students had science. No experiments today. Instead Mrs. Hartwell talked, and talked, and talked.

It wasn't very exciting . . . until Brandon
fell out of his chair.

Social studies, and then reading . . .
The afternoon crawled by. Everyone
looked their best sitting quietly in their
seats. But no one was smiling or
having fun.

"I don't think this day is ever going to end,"
Andy said, putting his head down on the desk.

Finally, Mrs. Hartwell told everyone to put away their books and papers.

The class cheered.

"It's time to do our chores and straighten up the room," Mrs. Hartwell said.

As students threw away trash, fed the class
pets, and straightened the books and art supplies,
Mrs. Hartwell kept a watchful eye, swooping in
to fix any potential mess.

When they were done, Mrs. Hartwell smiled. "Congratulations! You made it through the day, and you still look picture-perfect."

"Now it's my turn," she thought, finally getting a chance to look in the mirror. "Oh my!"

"Don't worry, I can fix it," Mrs. Hartwell reassured the class.

But just then, they got called down to the gym for pictures.

The students lined up to take their individual pictures. As each one waited their turn, Mrs. Hartwell helped them look their best.

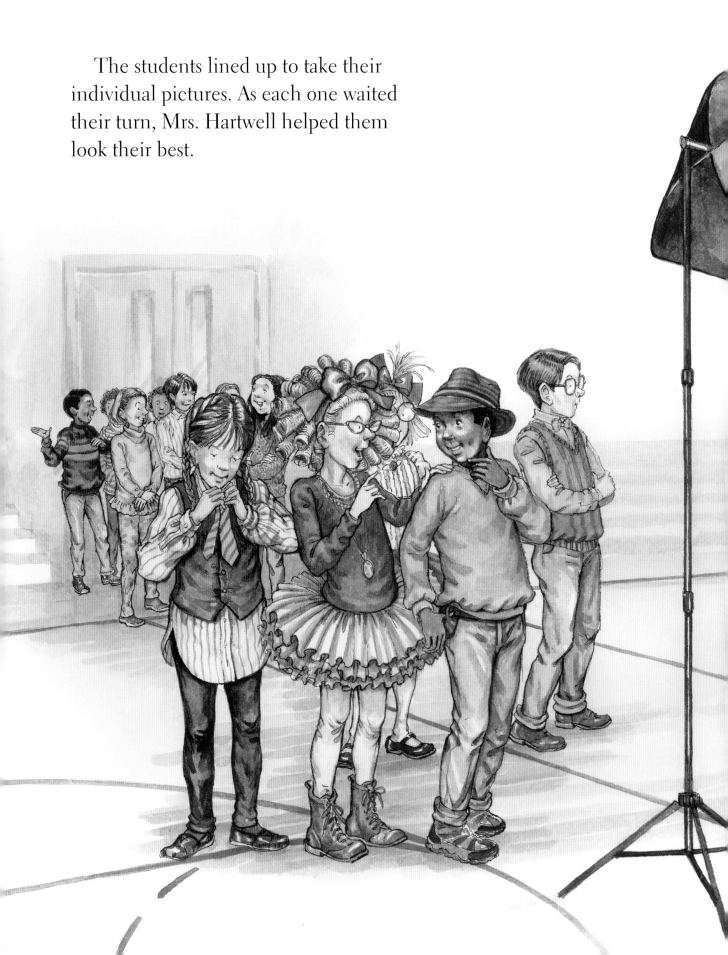

The students were glad to be done.

When it was time for the class picture,
Mrs. Hartwell called everyone back together.

"Oh no," she said. The class wasn't
picture-perfect anymore. "Don't worry, I can
fix it," she reassured them.

"We don't have time," said the photographer.

She snapped the picture
just as the bell rang.

Several weeks later, just before Mrs. Hartwell handed out the picture packets, she said, "I have to warn you. Our class picture didn't turn out as I planned."

The students looked worried.

Then Mrs. Hartwell laughed. "It turned out better."
The students looked confused.
"When I saw our class picture," Mrs. Hartwell said,
"I realized that there was nothing to fix because . . ."

". . . you're picture-perfect just the way you are!"

"We look like we do every day!" the students said.
"And that's how I like us best," Mrs. Hartwell replied with a smile.